This edition published by Parragon Books Ltd in 2014

Parragon Books Ltd
Chartist House
15–17 Trim Street
Bath BA1 1HA, UK
www.parragon.com

ISBN 978-1-4723-7982-5

Printed in China

Bath • New York • Cologne • Melbourne • Delhi
Hong Kong • Shenzhen • Singapore • Amsterdam

Andy loved his toys, and they loved him. Sheriff Woody, Buzz Lightyear, Jessie the cowgirl, Rex, Hamm and all the rest were happiest when they were off on one of Andy's wildly imaginative adventures. It didn't matter whether Andy pretended the toys had X-ray vision or superhuman strength, or whether he made them villains or heroes. The toys all agreed: simply being played with by a kid – by Andy – was the best feeling in the world.

But as Andy grew into a teenager, he played with the toys less and less. By the time he was preparing for college, the toys were very worried. What would happen to them? Woody tried to reassure everyone. Andy would just tuck them all in the attic for safekeeping, he explained.

Andy's mum had another idea, however. She suggested that Andy donate his old toys to a daycare centre.

"No one's going to want those," he told her. "They're junk."

The toys were shocked. Then Andy opened the toy box, scooped up Rex, Hamm, Slinky and Mr and Mrs Potato Head – and dumped them into a rubbish bag! He paused for a moment, looking at his two favourites, Buzz and Woody. Then, he dropped Woody into a box marked "**COLLEGE**" – and Buzz went into the rubbish bag, too!

At first, the toys thought they were headed for the bin. But in fact, Andy planned to put the bag in the attic. Then Andy's mum made a terrible mistake. She assumed the bag was rubbish and dumped it at the curb.

Frantic, Woody climbed out the window to help his friends. He was still looking for them when the bin lorry arrived. He watched in horror as the bin man hurled the bags into the back of the lorry and crushed the entire load with the lorry's compactor!

Then Woody noticed an upside-down recycling bin moving across Andy's driveway. His friends had escaped!

Inside the garage, the toys were hurt and confused. What would they do now that Andy had thrown them away?

Jessie had an idea: Go to the daycare centre! She convinced everyone to climb inside the box of old toys that Mum planned to donate.

Woody followed his friends into the box. He tried to explain about the rubbish bag mix-up, but the toys didn't believe him.

SLAM! Suddenly, Andy's mum shut the hatchback, got in, and started driving.

Woody had been hoping to lead everyone back to Andy, but Jessie convinced the group that wouldn't work. Didn't Woody understand that Andy didn't want them anymore?

Soon the receptionist at Sunnyside Daycare was carrying the box of toys down to the daycare centre's Butterfly Room.

While the children were playing, Andy's toys couldn't contain their excitement and spilled out onto the floor. The daycare toys welcomed them with open arms.

Friendliest of all was a big, pink bear who smelled like strawberries. "Welcome to Sunnyside!" he called warmly. "I'm Lots-o'-Huggin' Bear! But, please, call me Lotso!"

"Mr Lotso," asked Rex. "Do toys here get played with every day?"

"All day long," Lotso answered. "When the kids get old, new ones come in. No owners means no heartbreak."

To the toys, daycare was sounding better and better!

Lotso and a doll named Big Baby led the toys on a tour of Sunnyside before escorting them to their new home at Sunnyside: The Caterpillar Room.

Woody begged his friends not to stay. They belonged at Andy's house.

But Jessie and the others disagreed. "We can have a new life here, Woody," the cowgirl argued.

Woody could see his friends' minds were made up. Feeling sad and conflicted, he said good-bye.

He clambered onto the roof and used an old kite to propel himself over the daycare centre's walls. When he crash-landed a little while later, he was bruised, hatless and dangling by his pull-string from a tree branch.

The receptionist's daughter, Bonnie, ran over to the dangling cowboy and shoved him into her rucksack. Then she took him home.

Inside the Caterpillar Room, Andy's toys waited excitedly as footsteps thundered towards them. Suddenly, a crowd of toddlers burst into the room. They tangled Slinky's coil, dipped Jessie's hair in paint and covered Hamm with glitter and glue. They broke off Rex's tail, hammered with Buzz's head and stuck the Potato Heads' parts up their noses!

One of the toddlers threw Buzz onto a windowsill. He could see into the Butterfly Room . . . where a group of four and five-year-olds were playing gently with Lotso and the other daycare toys.

Buzz wondered: Why had Andy's toys been put in the Caterpillar room? The toddlers' play was too rough!

After the children went home, the toys tried to put themselves back together.

"Andy never played with us like that!" Rex exclaimed.

"I'll go talk to Lotso about moving us to the other room," said Buzz.

Then they discovered all the doors and windows were locked. Finally, Buzz escaped through an open transom above the door.

While he was gone, Mrs Potato Head started to see strange images, coming to her through the eye she'd lost back at Andy's house.

"Andy's looking in the attic," she said. "Why is he so upset?" She gasped. "I think he did mean to put us in the attic!"

Now that the toys realized their mistake, they knew they had to go home!

Buzz found some of the Sunnyside toys inside a vending machine, in the Teacher's Lounge. He overheard them talking – and learned that these toys knew how dangerous the Caterpillar Room was. Andy's toys had been sent there on purpose! Buzz tried to go and warn his friends, but he was captured.

When Lotso arrived, he was as friendly as ever. He even granted Buzz's request to be transferred to the Butterfly Room – on the condition that Buzz's friends stay behind.

"I can't accept," said Buzz. "We're a family. We stay together."

Suddenly, Lotso's attitude changed. With a cruel smile, he called for the Buzz Lightyear Instruction Manual. Then he ordered his gang to reset Buzz's switch to "Demo Mode."

When Lotso arrived in the Caterpillar Room, Andy's toys begged to leave.

"Here's the thing," the bear said, grinning nastily. "You ain't leaving Sunnyside." He wanted Andy's toys to stay with the littlest kids. Somebody had to endure their rough play, and it wasn't going to be Lotso's gang!

Then, suddenly, Buzz appeared and accused his old friends of being "minions of Zurg"!

Jessie and the others were shocked. What had happened to Buzz?

Lotso's gang herded Andy's toys into the room's wire cubbies. When Mr Potato Head fought back, Big Baby made him stay overnight in a covered sandbox out in the playground.

Lotso chuckled and left, leaving the captives under Buzz's stern guard. The happy daycare had turned into a grim prison!

Meanwhile, at Bonnie's house, Woody was actually having fun. The little girl had a great imagination, and her toys were very kind.

But then Woody discovered he was just a few streets from Andy's house!

"If you guys ever get to Sunnyside Daycare," said Woody, waving good-bye, "tell them Woody made it home."

The toys gasped. Chuckles, a toy clown, knew all about Sunnyside. Long ago, Chuckles explained, he, Lotso and Big Baby had belonged to a little girl named Daisy. One day, the toys were accidentally left behind during a trip. Lotso led them on a long journey home, but Daisy had already got a new pink bear. Heartbroken and furious, Lotso ripped off the pendant with Daisy's name on it that Big Baby always wore. Eventually, the trio ended up at Sunnyside – where Lotso became the daycare centre's bitter tyrant. Chuckles would have perished, except that Bonnie rescued him after he was broken.

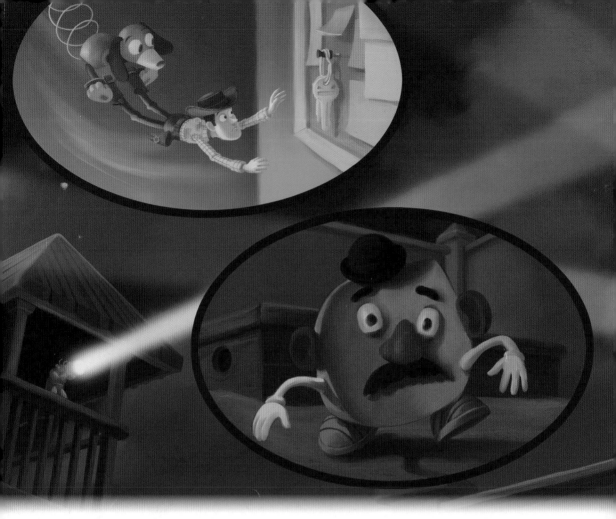

As much as Woody wanted to get home to Andy, he knew he couldn't leave his friends in Lotso's clutches. The next day, he hitched a ride to the daycare centre in Bonnie's rucksack.

The cowboy found his pals and told them how they could break out of Sunnyside. That night, the toys sprang into action. Woody and Slinky surprised the toy monkey who sat by the security monitors – and grabbed the daycare keys. Mr Potato Head distracted Big Baby while the others captured Buzz. Meanwhile, Barbie forced Ken to tell her about Buzz's instruction manual. Then she and the other toys attempted to reset Buzz's switch – but something went wrong. Now Buzz only spoke Spanish!

Despite the setback, everyone made it to their destination: the rubbish chute in the playground.

Woody and the rest of the toys climbed into the rubbish chute and slid down one by one. At the bottom, Slinky formed a bridge between the chute and the lid of the nearby bin so his friends could walk across to freedom.

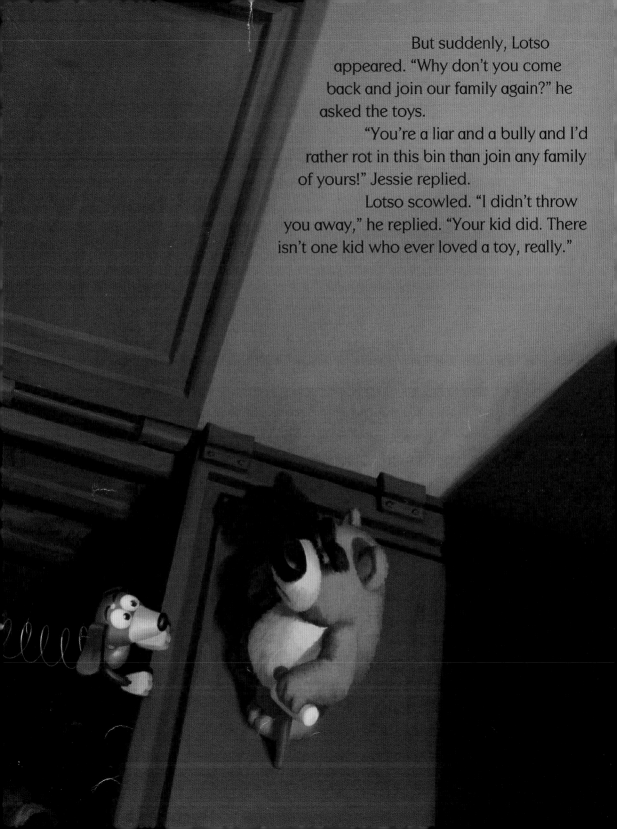

But suddenly, Lotso appeared. "Why don't you come back and join our family again?" he asked the toys.

"You're a liar and a bully and I'd rather rot in this bin than join any family of yours!" Jessie replied.

Lotso scowled. "I didn't throw you away," he replied. "Your kid did. There isn't one kid who ever loved a toy, really."

"What about Daisy?" Woody asked suddenly. "She lost you. By accident. She loved you!" He threw the old pendant that Chuckles had given him at the Lotso's feet.

"She never loved me!" Lotso exploded angrily. "She left me!"

Big Baby's eyes filled with tears as he thought about Daisy.

"You want your Mummy back? She never loved you!' Lotso shouted, and gave Big Baby a shove.

Big Baby had had enough. He hoisted Lotso into the air – and threw him into a big rubbish bin!

The daycare toys cheered. Things would be different at Sunnyside from now on.

"Come on! Hurry!" cried Woody, starting across the lid. He could hear a rubbish lorry rumbling towards them!

The toys followed, and climbed to safety on a wall.

Then Woody saw an Alien caught in between the bin lids. The cowboy ran back, but Lotso reached up and yanked Woody inside! The rest of Andy's toys jumped onto the lid and tried to pry it open, but the rubbish lorry lifted the container and tilted it upside down. Soon all the toys fell into the back of the rubbish lorry.

The truck rumbled forwards, then lurched to a stop. More rubbish rained down on them and a TV landed on top of Buzz. Incredibly, the blow turned him back into his old self!

Soon the lorry arrived at the Tri-County Landfill and dumped its load. **"The claaaaw!"** shouted the Aliens excitedly as they toddled off towards a crane in the distance.

Woody tried to go after them, but was cut off by a huge bulldozer. Rumbling, it pushed him and his friends towards an open pit.

The toys fell onto a conveyor belt that led to a shredder. But they soon discovered another conveyor belt above them that was magnetic. They grabbed onto whatever metal trash they could find and were lifted to safety.

Suddenly, they heard a cry for help. Lotso was trapped! Woody and Buzz dropped down and used a golf club to free him. The shredder was just inches away!

Woody grabbed Lotso's paw, the golf club flew towards the magnet and all three were lifted to safety. Next they dropped down to their friends, who were on another conveyor belt far below.

They thought they saw daylight at the end of this belt – but suddenly realized it was actually an incinerator!

Lotso managed to find the Emergency Stop Button that could save them all, but instead of pushing it, he hesitated. Then a cruel smirk came across his face and he ran off.

Woody and his friends tumbled towards the fire, determined to face it the best way they knew how: together.

Then, suddenly, a large shadow passed over them. A giant crane lowered its jaws and scooped the toys up and away from the scorching fire. Inside the crane's cab, the Aliens steered their friends over the landfill and dropped them gently to the ground.

Now the toys had to get Woody home before Andy left for college. Luckily, they spotted their neighbourhood rubbish man nearby, just climbing into his truck. The toys hurried forwards, ready to hitch a ride home.

Lotso found his way onto a different truck. But he wouldn't be hopping off anytime soon! He had been taped to the front of a lorry!

Woody and the gang arrived home as Andy was loading up the car. They had made it just in time!

Woody headed for a box marked "**COLLEGE**," while the others climbed into an "**ATTIC**" box. Before they separated, Woody and Buzz shook hands.

"You know where to find us, Cowboy," Buzz said finally.

Inside the "**COLLEGE**" box, Woody looked at a photo of Andy with all his toys. The cowboy knew that – no matter where any of them went – they would always carry the memories of their time together. But as he sat in the box alone, something did not feel quite right.

Suddenly, Woody had an idea. He jumped out of the box, hastily wrote something on a sticky note, and placed it on the attic box.

When Andy arrived to grab the last boxes, he read the note. Then he opened the attic box and got a wonderful surprise – his toys hadn't been thrown away, after all!

"Hey, Mum," he shouted. "Do you really think I should donate these?"

"It's up to you," she called back.

A little while later, Andy pulled up to Bonnie's house.

"Someone told me you're really good with toys," Andy said to the little girl.

As Andy introduced his toys to Bonnie, he was startled to find Woody in the box. He wasn't supposed to be there!

"My cowboy!" Bonnie cried happily.

Though it was hard for him, Andy let Woody stay with Bonnie, too. From the hug she gave the cowboy, Andy could see that she already loved him.

Back in the car, Andy took one last look at a smiling Bonnie surrounded by his toys.

"Thanks, guys," he said quietly before pulling away.

Bonnie went inside for lunch, and the toys watched Andy disappear down the street.

"So long, partner," said Woody.

Buzz and the others gathered around him. Their life with Andy was ending, but their adventures with Bonnie had just begun.